A GIFT
FROM
THE PEOPLE OF THE REPUBLIC OF FRANCE
TO THE PEOPLE OF THE UNITED STATES.

THIS STATUE
OF
LIBERTY ENLIGHTENING THE WORLD

COMMEMORATES THE ALLIANCE OF THE TWO NATIONS
IN ACHIEVING THE INDEPENDENCE
OF THE
UNITED STATES OF AMERICA,
AND
ATTESTS THEIR ABIDING FRIENDSHIP.

AUGUSTE BARTHOLDI.
SCULPTOR.

INAUGURATED
OCTOBER 28TH 1886.

THE STATUE OF LIBERTY

LEONARD EVERETT FISHER

Holiday House / New York

Souvenir

PROGRAMME

Of the Unveiling
to the Government

and Presentation
of the United States

Of the Bartholdi

Conceived 1865.

Completed 1886.

Statue of Liberty

ILLUMINATED BY THE AMERICAN SYSTEM OF ELECTRIC LIGHTING

AT LIBERTY ISLAND,

New York Bay,
OCTOBER 28TH, 1886.

PRICE. 10 CENTS.

Leaden daylight broke cold and drizzly on Thursday, October 28, 1886. A shot fired from the U.S.S. *Tennessee,* anchored in Upper New York Bay, echoed on the Hudson and East River tides. In the dreary, bone-chilling wet air, French sculptor Frédéric-Auguste Bartholdi's *Liberty Enlightening the World*—better known as the Statue of Liberty—rose above its great stone pedestal on Bedloe's Island and waited to be received by the American public. By noon, a crushing, high-spirited mass of people was straining to witness Grover Cleveland, the president of the United States, dedicate the soaring copper and iron statue, which was now partly hidden by mist and rain.

Seen from the tip of Manhattan, "Miss Liberty" was a vague silhouette nearly two miles away. Yet there she stood, her great torch-bearing right arm thrust skyward, challenging the fog and rain in a timely gesture of eternal liberty.

The crowd could barely see the huge French flag that covered her face. The driving rain and gloomy clouds all but erased the view. On Bedloe's Island, the soggy wind rippled the flag's waterlogged folds in an endless slow-motion rhythm. From time to time, the great red, white and blue banner of the French Republic blew against the statue's serious face, outlining its classic features to the gathering assembly of invited guests at its feet.

In the water around Bedloe's Island, a massive naval parade was staged in celebration of Miss Liberty's unveiling. Farther north, more than a million soaking spectators cheered themselves hoarse while watching a parade along Fifth Avenue and down Broadway. Bands, floats, military units, politicians, associations, clubs and societies—some twenty thousand marchers in all—strutted past the reviewing stands.

At midafternoon Frédéric-Auguste Bartholdi was high up in the statue's torch—some three-hundred feet above ground—waiting for a signal to release the tricolor flag and complete the

The cover of the souvenir program for the dedication ceremony of the Statue of Liberty, October 29, 1886, THE BETTMAN ARCHIVE, INC.

unveiling. This would be followed by President Cleveland's remarks. Even at that breathless moment, Bartholdi, the creator of the world's largest statue, did not have a clear, bright view of his *Liberty Enlightening the World*. He had arrived from France only a few days before, accompanied by his wife, Jeanne-Emilie; the builder of the Suez Canal, Ferdinand-Marie de Lesseps; and Lesseps' daughter, Tototte. Their ship, the *Bretagne*, sailed into New York Harbor through a thick fog. The statue loomed as a dim ghostly shape. The view was somewhat improved the next day, when the Bartholdi party was taken on a misty sail around the harbor. But still, Bartholdi had not seen his creation clearly. Nor would he today.

The gray weather seemed to underscore the touch of uneasiness that drifted around France's wonderful gift to the American public—the Statue of Liberty. While the public cheered and cannons boomed their salute on this gala day of dedication, the gigantic statue of Woman symbolizing "liberty enlightening the world" did not stand all that comfortably on its brand-new pedestal.

In nineteenth-century America, a pedestal was where a woman belonged, to be adored and worshiped, out of harm's way, pure and unreachable—a goddess in every respect. Women were not expected to participate in politics and business. Nor were they expected to contribute to any political or commercial process affecting the nation or themselves. The nineteenth century was a world run by men. As if to insure that a woman's role remain limited, women could not vote. And it would not be until 1920—a generation removed from the Statue of Liberty project—that the Nineteenth Amendment to the United States Constitution would give all American women the right to vote nationwide.

It was no surprise then that only two women were invited to be present on Bedloe's Island when President Grover Cleveland proclaimed that "a stream of light shall pierce the darkness of igno-

FRANK LESLIE'S
ILLUSTRATED
NEWSPAPER

Entered according to Act of Congress, in the year 1886, by Mrs. Frank Leslie, in the Office of the Librarian of Congress at Washington.—Entered at the Post Office, New York, N.Y., as Second-class Matter.

No. 1,622.—Vol. LXIII.]   NEW YORK—FOR THE WEEK ENDING OCTOBER 23, 1886.   [Price, 10 Cents. $4.00 Yearly. 15 Weeks, $1.00.

NEW YORK.—COMPLETING THE BARTHOLDI STATUE OF LIBERTY—VIEW OF THE INTERIOR OF THE UPPER PORTION OF THE STATUE.

FROM A SKETCH BY A STAFF ARTIST.—SEE PAGE 149.

rance." They were Jeanne-Emilie Bartholdi, the sculptor's wife, and Tototte de Lesseps. Neither woman was an American. Those who arranged the inaugural ceremonies would not vouch for a woman's safety in a crowd.

The New York State Woman Suffragette Association was enraged. The members of the association chartered a boat and sailed their protest within earshot of those participating in the Bedloe's Island ceremonies. There, at the island's edge, they screamed their grievances and tried to rattle the almost all-male crowd. William M. Evarts, the principal speaker, was hardly disturbed by this seagoing outburst. Still, he paused long enough in his long-winded speech for an aide to believe he had finished. The aide, as previously instructed, sent a signal to Bartholdi that Evarts had finished. Now was the time to unveil Miss Liberty, and Bartholdi did—about an hour too soon.

By the end of the day, however, the long and often difficult road to place the colossal monument in New York Harbor had come to an end. Now the Statue of Liberty could take its place beside the flag, the Liberty Bell and the bald eagle as a national symbol. Almost instantly, the copper-colored Miss Liberty, shining like a new penny, became recognized around the world as a symbol for the true meaning of America and the best that America had to offer—liberty, freedom and opportunity. Standing so tall at the entrance to New York, the greatest port in the world, the Statue of Liberty offered hope to all the miserable souls on the globe who would reach for American democracy and citizenship.

Strangely, the Statue of Liberty was not dedicated as a national monument in October 1886. It was not until 1924—thirty-eight years later—that Miss Liberty was officially proclaimed a national monument.

The idea for so gigantic a project began in 1865. Interestingly enough, it did not begin in the United States but in France, under the reign of Emperor Napoléon III and the Second French Empire.

By 1865, the American Civil War had ended. Four years of disunity and bloody battles between the North and South were over. Andrew Johnson was now president, following the shocking murder of Abraham Lincoln. There was no longer a single law in the land making slavery legal. Unlike France, America had a government without a king or emperor. American leaders, including presidents, all held office by popular election. The United States could now begin to live up to the ideals it professed in the Declaration of Independence, 1776: ". . . that all Men are created equal, that they are endowed by their Creator with certain unalienable Rights . . . Life, Liberty, and the Pursuit of Happiness."

The idea of liberty was an important American building block on which was fashioned the freest nation of people in the world. It was not perfect. But it would try to be. These ideals were an inspiration to a group of Frenchmen who were unhappy with their empire. They dreamed of the day that France would rid itself of Napoléon III, the emperor, and have a government run by the people.

In 1865, this politically active group was meeting regularly for dinner to discuss the state of French affairs. Frédéric-Auguste Bartholdi, a thirty-one-year-old popular sculptor, was one of the participants. So was the legal scholar and constitutional lawyer Professor Edouard-René LeFebvre de Laboulaye. At one of the dinners, Laboulaye suggested that a "monument" be built to bring Americans and Frenchmen closer together since they shared common ideals of "Liberty, Equality and Fraternity." Laboulaye imagined a new constitution for France once Napoléon III and his government were toppled—a constitution modeled after the

Frédéric-Auguste Bartholdi, NPS

13

American constitution.

"If a monument were to be built in America as a memorial to their independence," offered Laboulaye, "I think it very natural if it were built by united efforts, if it were a common work of both nations."

The idea churned in the mind of Laboulaye. But it took four more years for the grandeur of it to settle on Bartholdi. The always-busy Bartholdi had a more pressing project. He wanted to erect a colossal statue that could also be a lighthouse at the entrance of the soon-to-be-completed Suez Canal. The design of the hundred-mile-long canal was the work of French engineers working under the direction of Ferdinand-Marie de Lesseps. Bartholdi's interest in the canal stemmed from a visit he had made to Egypt early in his career in 1856. It was then, after viewing the gigantic pyramids and Sphinx, that the idea of someday creating enormous public statues crossed his mind. Bartholdi already had some experience with large-scale sculpture.

Frédéric-Auguste Bartholdi was born into a wealthy landowning family on August 2, 1834, in the town of Colmar, Alsace Province, France. He was a boy when his father died. His doting mother, Charlotte, encouraged him to study painting in Paris. Paris, the art center of Europe, was alive with artists who would leave their mark on the world—Delacroix, Courbet, Millet and Corot, among others. But in 1856, twenty-two-year-old Bartholdi was commissioned by the town of Colmar to create a statue of General Jean Rapp, a hero who lived during the time of Napoléon I. With the commission, Bartholdi's enthusiasm for painting pictures was overshadowed by his desire to create large sculptural works.

The statue of General Rapp, dragged through the streets of Paris to be seen at an exhibition before shipment to Colmar, was twenty-six feet high from its pedestal base to the very top. It

Edouard-René LeFebvre de Laboulaye. His grandson, François de Laboulaye, is a former French ambassador to the United States. NPS

14

would not fit through the salon doors. While twenty-six feet may not seem outrageously high today, the low-scale cityscape of mid-nineteenth-century Paris made it seem enormous. Bartholdi's itch to create large works had begun, and it would preoccupy him for the rest of his life.

Bartholdi worked for two years, 1867–1869, devising a model of his statue for the Suez Canal in Egypt. The idea for such a gigantic project had ancient roots. Bartholdi knew about one of the Seven Wonders of the Ancient World—Alexander's Lighthouse, also called the Pharos of Alexandria. Before it was destroyed by an earthquake in the 1300s, it stood four hundred feet high on the island of Pharos, near Alexandria, the city in Egypt founded in 332 B.C. by Alexander the Great. Built during the third century B.C., the Pharos of Alexandria had stood for one thousand years.

Another of the Seven Wonders of the Ancient World that Bartholdi knew about was the Colossus of Rhodes, a hundred-foot-high statue of the sun god Helios. It was built in the harbor of the island of Rhodes about 280 B.C. Like Alexander's Lighthouse, the Colossus of Rhodes was destroyed by an earthquake—in 224 A.D. It had lasted for five hundred years. Bartholdi also knew about a large statue on Lake Maggiore in northern Italy. It was of Saint Charles Borromeo, the sixteenth-century archbishop of Milan. What interested Bartholdi about the Italian piece was the technique used to create it—copper repoussé. In this technique, thin copper sheets are hammered against hard plaster molds that take on the shape of the statue. The molds are made by forming wet plaster around shapes sculpted from clay, and allowing the plaster to dry. When the hammering has been finished, the newly crafted sheets of copper must be connected to a supporting skeleton or framework of iron rods called the armature. Seen from the outside, a statue done in copper repoussé looks solid. But other than its iron skeleton, it is hollow inside.

Alexander's Lighthouse, LEONARD EVERETT FISHER

With all this in mind, Bartholdi traveled to Egypt in 1869 for the opening of the Suez Canal, where he hoped to convince Ismā'īl Pasha, the Egyptian viceroy, to commission him to erect the statue. Bartholdi's idea was to create a colossal figure of an Egyptian peasant woman bearing a torch in her right hand. The figure was to be a symbol of modern Egypt with the lamp of enlightenment held aloft and out to the rest of the area's less developed countries. Bartholdi was appealing to Ismā'īl Pasha's pride, if not his ego. It did not work. The pasha could accept French financial aid in rebuilding the ancient cities of Cairo and Alexandria. He could accept French skill in building a canal that would benefit the Egyptian economy and give Egypt an important place among the modern nations of the world. But the Egyptian ruler would not or could not allow a Greek-looking statue at the Suez Canal entrance, designed and built by a westerner—a Frenchman—and taller than Egypt's own treasured ancient monuments, the Sphinx and the pyramids. Such a figure, in Ismā'īl Pasha's eyes, would be more of a monument to Bartholdi and France than to him and Egypt. The pasha rejected Bartholdi and his ideas on the excuse that the light on the statue should be carried on top of the head of the figure in the manner that peasant Egyptian women carry their bundles. He insisted on this instead of Bartholdi's vision of a torch in the figure's hand or a fiery beacon shining from the statue's forehead.

Despite his failure in Egypt, Bartholdi was not discouraged. If the Old World would not have his colossal ideas, then perhaps the New World would be more willing. Laboulaye's still-simmering idea of a French-American monument now boiled in Bartholdi's mind. What failed in Egypt would succeed in America. Bartholdi turned all his energies toward that end—toward his "American project." At Laboulaye's urging, Bartholdi made plans to go to America to awaken interest among important Americans for this

Bartholdi's vision for a statue at the entrance of the Suez Canal, LEONARD EVERETT FISHER

unique project. It was both Laboulaye's and Bartholdi's intention that such a monument be completed and set on its American pedestal by 1876—in time to celebrate one hundred years of American independence.

The young, enthusiastic sculptor would have to be patient, however. A conflict was brewing between France and Prussia, the leading German state. The Prussian chancellor, Otto von Bismarck, anxious to weld all the German states into a single, strong country, needed a war with France to accomplish his purpose. By threatening to make a German prince king of Spain, he schemed to have France start the war. France could live with German states on her eastern frontier, but not on her southern border, too. Such an alliance and arrangement would also threaten the coast of western France. In effect, France would be surrounded by powerful military forces of the German states and their ally, Spain. These and other diplomatic moves, designed to make France angry, succeeded. France attacked Prussia on July 15, 1870.

Frédéric-Auguste Bartholdi rushed from Paris to his native Colmar. A major in the French National Guard, he wanted to attend to the safety of his mother, now in the direct path of advancing Prussian armies. France had been losing battles everywhere. She seemed confused and was no match for the well-trained Prussians. There, at Colmar, Bartholdi organized a pitiful group of soldiers to defend the town after the bulk of the French army had surrendered to the Prussians at nearby Sedan, after Emperor Napoléon III himself had been captured and made a prisoner, and after Paris had fallen. It was Bartholdi's fate to surrender Colmar to the Prussians.

Under the terms of the Treaty of Frankfurt, May 10, 1871, which ended the war, France had to give up the provinces of Alsace and Lorraine (including Bartholdi's hometown, Colmar). Also, France had to pay a huge sum of money to the German

Bartholdi's mother, Charlotte, NPS

states and accept an army of occupation until the money was paid. As a result of the French defeat, the French emperor was replaced by a president, which gave the French people a republican form of government; and the German states under Prussian leadership became unified as a single country and Europe's most powerful nation.

Bartholdi was intensely concerned with the loss of Alsace and his town of Colmar to the Prussians. In his eyes, Colmar had to be liberated one day and returned to France. Bartholdi's patriotism, already on fire, unleashed all his noble ideas of liberty. And someday he would express his patriotic longing for his lost town of Colmar, together with his dreams of monumental sculpture in a single-minded idea, the Statue of Liberty. With an elected president now governing France from Versailles, the temporary capital, ideas of liberty flew on every French wind. It was time for Bartholdi to present his and Laboulaye's ideas to the American people.

Armed with letters of introduction that would lead him to President Ulysses S. Grant, editor Horace Greeley, poet Henry Wadsworth Longfellow, United States Senator Charles Sumner of Massachusetts, philanthropist Peter Cooper, painter John La Farge, architect Henry H. Richardson, and Philadelphia newspaper publisher Colonel John W. Forney, Bartholdi arrived in New York City aboard the *Periere* on June 21, 1871.

During his five-month visit, the first of four such visits he would make to the United States, Bartholdi traveled across the country to San Francisco and back again. Everywhere he journeyed—New Haven, Boston, Detroit, Chicago, Omaha, Denver, Salt Lake City, Cincinnati, Washington, D.C., and other places—he did all he could to win the support of the American people for a statue commemorating the ideal of liberty.

During the trip, Bartholdi was struck, if not overwhelmed, by

Bartholdi's early terracotta model
of the Statue of Liberty,
MUSEUM OF THE CITY OF NEW YORK

the country's immense size, its bursting energy and its friendliness. He also thought that Americans were so intent on building a country on such a grand scale that they did not take the time to study and appreciate art. There was some enthusiasm for his ideas, but not enough to demand that a colossal Statue of Liberty be placed in New York Harbor in time to celebrate the Centennial of American Independence five years later. Bartholdi was convinced that New York Harbor should be the site of the statue. In fact, he had surveyed the harbor and concluded that Bedloe's Island, located in the Upper Bay, was the only place for a Statue of Liberty.

The twelve-acre island once belonged to a Dutch settler named Isaack Bedloo. Bedloo had bought the island from the Mohegan Indians, who did not think it important. From time to time it was called Lesser Island, Love Island or Great Oyster Island. Its name was changed to Bedlow, and Bedloe, long before the United States government took it over in 1800 and built a fort on it. The fort—Fort Wood—was named later after Eleazar Wood, an army officer killed in the War of 1812. The star-shaped fort had numerous functions until it was abandoned as a military post in 1937. The island was not called Liberty Island, its current name, until 1956. But it had been Bartholdi's wish from the very beginning of his "American project" that the island site of *Liberty Enlightening the World* should be called Liberty Island. In any case, the island was used as an ammunition dump during the Civil War, a military hospital, and later served as a U.S. Army communications center.

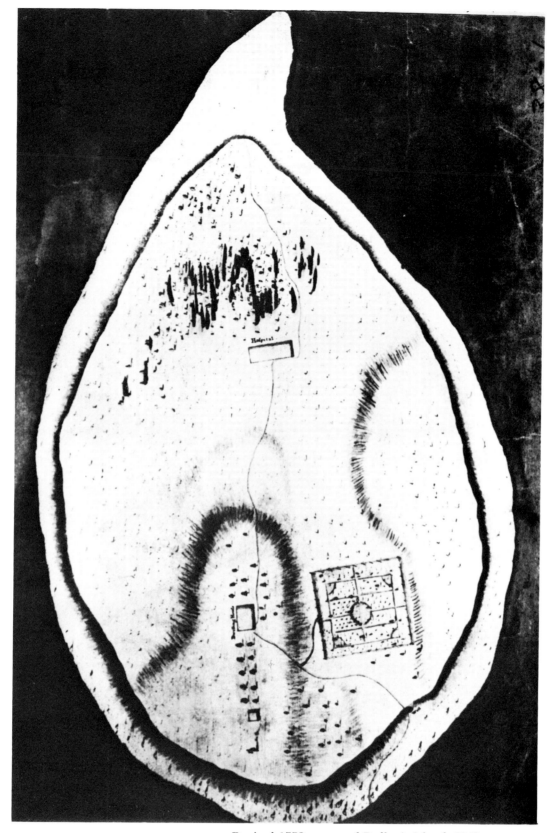

Revised 1772 survey of Bedloe's Island, 1843, NPS

One of Bartholdi's original drawings of *Liberty Enlightening the World* on Bedloe's Island, circa 1875, NPS

25

Bartholdi had come to America not only to promote the idea of a Statue of Liberty but to convince Americans that the project should be a shared event: The French people would provide the statue; the American people would provide the pedestal on which the statue would stand. He returned to France without firm agreements from either the American government or private citizens. The general feeling in America was that if this was to be a gift from the people of France to the people of the United States, then France should be responsible for both statue and pedestal. More moderate voices said that France would have to begin the project and show the average American and the country's wealthy citizens that this was indeed a worthy project to be shared by France and America.

Bartholdi was hardly put off by his failure to rouse the American people into giving official recognition to his project. He could not even be sure that the American public would accept such a gift in the first place. Yet, moved by his own enthusiasm for America and encouraged by what he rightly believed to have been a warm and friendly reception in America, Bartholdi began to work out his grand scheme for *Liberty Enlightening the World.*

As luck would have it, Bartholdi was interrupted in his "American project" by a commission that would heighten both French and American interest in the proposed Statue of Liberty. Louis-Adolphe Thiers, the French president, commissioned Bartholdi to create a statue of the Marquis de Lafayette, whose active support of the American fight for independence was still a cherished memory in America nearly one hundred years after the Revolutionary War. The statue would be a French gift to the people of New York City in appreciation of their warm support of France in her recent war with Prussia. The statue, to be set on a pedestal in Union Square, the center of the city in the 1870s, would be dedicated sometime during the centennial celebration in 1876, as indeed it was.

One of Bartholdi's working drawings, circa 1875, NPS

27

Meanwhile, as Bartholdi began to work on *Liberty,* and completed *Lafayette,* excitement over these projects mounted on both sides of the Atlantic Ocean. The time was right to organize a fund-raising campaign. Accordingly, in 1874, Laboulaye and Bartholdi founded the Union Franco-Americaine Committee to manage the entire Statue of Liberty project. But it was not until the fall of 1875 that actual fund-raising began, too late to have a colossal statue on Bedloe's Island by 1876.

No matter; enthusiasm charged the air. A gala dinner was held in Paris on November 6, 1875. The dining room of the Hôtel du Louvre was festooned with French and American flags and jammed with important persons of both countries. American-French friendship was toasted throughout the long evening. The names of Lafayette and Benjamin Franklin were on everyone's lips. It was Benjamin Franklin, the American minister to France

Marquis de Lafayette and Benjamin Franklin,
LEONARD EVERETT FISHER

during the Revolutionary War, who brought France to the side of the American colonists. Some money was raised, and other contributions were pledged, to create the 151-foot-1-inch figure of *Liberty Enlightening the World,* the statue that would grace New York Harbor with a French presence and unite both France and the United States in ideals of liberty and eternal friendship.

The following spring, 1876, at a gala concert organized in Paris to raise money for the "American project," Laboulaye told the fashionable audience who had come to hear the *Liberty* Cantata, choral music composed for the occasion by Charles-François Gounod, "This Statue of Liberty . . . will preserve the precious memories which are links between the two nations; it will preserve among future generations . . . the eternal friendship of the United States and France." Gounod's *Liberty* Cantata would not be heard again for 109 years. Its second performance, sung by the Schola Cantorum of New York, was heard on April 11, 1985, at Lincoln Center's Alice Tully Hall in New York City.

A few weeks later, in May 1876, Bartholdi arrived in Philadelphia to attend the nation's birthday party at the Centennial Exposition. Not one to wait for things to happen, the compulsive Bartholdi had already begun to construct the massive *Liberty* in France early in 1876. The actual labor of building so huge a work of art was given to the Paris firm of Gaget, Gauthier et Cie. And it was in these workshops that parts of the Statue of Liberty had nearly been completed by the time Bartholdi arrived in Philadelphia. Bartholdi did not personally fashion the immense statue. He created small models in his private studio as early as 1870. These models were redone in successively larger clay and plaster forms before the final work was completed. Some of the steps in the complicated process were done by Gaget, Gauthier. Some were not. The firm of Moudinet & Becher created a full-scale clay model of the head before committing the final work to Gaget,

Bartholdi in his Paris studio, 1892, NPS

30

Gauthier. Dozens of workmen, all familiar with the various steps in creating the hollow copper sculpture, did the day-to-day labor.

The statue itself, comprised of three hundred separate sheets, was being constructed according to Bartholdi's design. The sheets were made of copper, measuring no more than $\frac{3}{32}$ of an inch (a little thicker than $\frac{1}{16}$ of an inch). The technique Bartholdi used to mold the statue's more-than-three-hundred sheets was repoussé, the very same method used to construct the statue of Saint Charles Borromeo that he had seen in Italy in 1869. Bartholdi had looked at the Italian monument on his return from Egypt with his rejected drawings for the Suez Canal statue. The repoussé technique was suitable for larger-scale public works. Once the copper was hammered into shape against the plaster molds, it was rigid, lightweight, easily dismantled and reassembled, and easily transported. The whole of the statue's copper "skin" would have to be bolted firmly in place to an iron skeletal armature, to remain rigid and stable.

(*on this and facing page*) Interior scenes at Gaget, Gauthier et Cie, as workmen labored to create the Statue of Liberty, NPS

The designing of the armature for the Statue of Liberty could not be a hit-or-miss affair. It had to be a perfectly calculated piece of structural engineering that would provide a permanent, secure and safe support for the very thin statue. The work of designing the armature belonged to Alexandre-Gustave Eiffel, a brilliant French structural engineer. Within a few short years, Eiffel would design his own unique piece of sculpture, the Eiffel Tower. The great iron skeletal structure on Paris's Champ de Mars would rise 984 feet above the city in 1889, to mark the French contribution on the site of the World's Fair. An incredible feat of structural engineering, and at the time the world's tallest structure, it remains today—along with the Statue of Liberty—one of the world's most familiar sights.

Eiffel's armature for the 450,000-pound Miss Liberty permitted the statue to contain a series of inside staircases. The stairs would make it possible for workmen to maintain the condition and safety of the iron armature that held the "skin"; it would also enable visitors and tourists to climb high into Miss Liberty's head, where windows would open onto panoramic vistas. Even the torch would be reachable from inside.

In August 1876, several months after Bartholdi arrived in Philadelphia, the statue's right hand bearing the torch was exhibited at the Centennial Exposition. It was used to rally support for the great gift that the American people still had not officially accepted. It was also used to raise money to continue the statue's construction. For an admission fee of fifty cents, a visitor could climb up into the hand and torch, and out onto the balcony that surrounded the torch. The piece was later removed to New York City, where it could be seen and visited on Madison Avenue and Twenty-third Street. Two years later, in 1878, the statue's head and shoulders were similarly exhibited in Paris, where again its chief function was to raise money for the continuation of the

Schematic drawing of the staircases
inside the statue, LEONARD EVERETT FISHER

project. It was here that former president Ulysses S. Grant saw the
head for the first time while on a trip around the world. He also
visited the studios and workshops where the Statue of Liberty was
being created. The hand and torch, which had been in America

Miss Liberty's head exhibited in Paris, 1878, NPS

for eight years, were sent back to the Paris workshops in 1884, destined to return to America with the finished statue.

Bartholdi returned to Paris himself in January 1877. He had spent nine months frantically promoting the Statue of Liberty as a French gift. Before he left, the United States Congress voted to accept the gift of the Statue of Liberty from the people of France. In addition, Congress authorized funds to maintain the statue once it was finished. And most importantly, one hundred well-known Americans formed the "American Committee" to raise money to build the Statue of Liberty pedestal. At last, the American people had committed themselves to the project—a project that would now be shared by France and the United States. The Bedloe's Island site was authorized by Congress a month later, on February 22, 1877, George Washington's birthday.

In all these respects, Bartholdi's trip was a resounding success. Thousands of people visited Liberty's hand and torch and would continue to do so for eight years while the project stumbled forward. However, lack of funds, misinformation, suspicion, and the stinginess of New York's wealthy citizens did much to delay the effort.

Ignoring the fundamental ideals of the Founding Fathers, some Americans were chiefly concerned with their own immediate interests. They feared that raising such a colossal symbol of liberty in the world's greatest port, New York, would cause unrest among the working classes. Many of these working-class Americans were recent immigrants who had come to America seeking the liberty represented by the statue. By forming labor unions, they were already threatening upper-class control over their lives. Among those at the "top" who did not want to contribute money for building the statue's pedestal were the Vanderbilts, the Goulds, the Morgans and Grover Cleveland himself.

Before he was president, Cleveland was the governor of New

President Grover Cleveland, COURTESY OF THE
NEW YORK HISTORICAL SOCIETY, NEW YORK CITY

38

York (1882–1884). During that time, he vetoed more legislation to save the taxpayers from overspending than any other holder of high office. Grover Cleveland's action to protect the taxpayer by not spending public funds for public projects was well-meaning. He believed it showed that he was a responsible administrator who had the people's best interests in mind. Still, Cleveland's veto of a bill to provide funds for the pedestal came amid a growing atmosphere of mistrust regarding the proposed presence of the Statue of Liberty in New York Harbor. It was an atmosphere that had been growing ever since the campaign was started to raise money for the pedestal in January 1877. Poet Henry Wadsworth Longfellow suggested to Bartholdi that a New York statue should be paid for by New Yorkers. He did not see it as a national monument and seemed to be suspicious of France's generosity and motives.

There were those who believed that a fraud was in the making. During the display of Miss Liberty's hand and torch at Philadelphia's Centennial Exposition in 1876, the *New York Times* attacked Bartholdi. It glibly charged that his singular vision was not for liberty as much as it was for lining his pockets with money at the expense of the American people. The ill-advised article, riddled with untruths, indirectly libeled some of the most respected families of France who were the chief supporters of the Statue of Liberty proposals—the Lafayettes, Rochambeaus, Laboulayes, Tocquevilles and others. Bartholdi, always the diplomat, raised no public outcry of hurt and indignation. Dismayed but undaunted, he stated his case in the Phildelphia *Press* of October 5, 1876. He conveyed both his and his country's sincerity and honesty, trusting the American people to know the difference between wild accusations and truth. The *Press* was squarely in the French camp. It was published by Colonel John W. Forney, one of the Statue of Liberty's chief backers. As far as the vast majority

The unveiling of the statue of Lafayette in New York City, 1876, LEONARD EVERETT FISHER

of Philadelphians were concerned, if the Statue of Liberty was to be rejected by New Yorkers, it could be erected in Philadelphia instead.

Bartholdi seemed to be everywhere at once, causing flutters of excitement on his constant travels between New York, Philadelphia and Washington, D.C. His name and project were in the newspapers nearly every day. Liberty's hand and torch were a chief attraction at the Philadelphia exposition.

In September 1876, Bartholdi attended the noisy festivities of the unveiling of his statue of Lafayette in New York City. It helped to focus even more attention on the Liberty project.

The Lafayette project was a near disaster. When the statue of Lafayette first arrived in New York, packed in crates, New Yorkers had not raised the money for a pedestal upon which to mount this first French gift. Bartholdi, on his frequent trips between Philadelphia and New York during the summer of 1876,

42

begged the French community of New York to provide the funds for the pedestal. They did. The statue took its place among the public treasures of New York, where it can still be seen in Union Square, at Park Avenue South and Fifteenth Street.

In addition to designing the statue of Lafayette for New York, Bartholdi designed a fountain especially for the French exhibit at the Philadelphia Centennial Exposition. It would be permanently installed in Washington, D.C., afterward. The entire country seemed to be awakening to Bartholdi and to the idea of having the "great goddess Liberty" with a blazing torch in New York Harbor. Only various groups of American artists seemed to receive him coolly and without encouragement whenever he appeared at their dinners to describe his liberty project. Nevertheless, it turned out not to matter what American artists thought, since by January 1877 the people of the United States, speaking through Congress, had told the people of France that they wanted Bartholdi's Statue of Liberty. And that was that.

Amid all these comings and goings, Bartholdi found the time to marry Jeanne-Emilie Baheux de Puysieux in Newport, Rhode Island. The energy of the man was boundless. Bartholdi had met Jeanne-Emilie in Newport at the home of his friend John La Farge, the American painter, on his first trip in 1871. Jeanne-Emilie returned to her native France but came back to America in 1876 to marry Bartholdi. It was not long after their return to Paris in January 1877, that romantic rumors drifted around the French capital that the arms of the Statue of Liberty were being modeled after the arms of the beautiful Jeanne-Emilie. Parisians had already decided that Bartholdi's mother, Charlotte, was the model for the face of Miss Liberty.

With the Bartholdis back in Paris after such an eventful trip, it was assumed that money for the statue's pedestal would come pouring in. It did not. There were some funds, but not enough.

Jeanne-Emilie Baheux de Puysieux,
Bartholdi's wife, NPS

Despite the U.S. government's approval of the gift, authorization of maintenance funds, and permission to use Bedloe's Island as the statue's site, both Congress and the State of New York refused to contribute any money for pedestal construction. The country's millionaires, most of whom lived in the New York area, all but turned their backs on the statue. What little money had been collected was not enough to bring the Statue of Liberty to New York from Paris and put it on a pedestal. There were those who loudly argued that if the French people wanted to give the American people a statue, they—the French people—should provide the pedestal, too. The American Committee, formed in January 1877 to raise money for the pedestal, and headed by William M. Evarts, a prominent New York lawyer, achieved little progress.

It remained for immigrant Joseph Pulitzer, publisher of the St. Louis *Post-Dispatch* and the New York *World,* to begin a grass-roots campaign to raise money for the pedestal. In an editorial on

CONTRIBUTIONS!!
FOR BARTHOLDI'S
STATUE OF

45

March 14, 1883, Pulitzer called the inability to fund the pedestal a "national disgrace." He blamed the New York millionaires for their refusal to contribute. The millionaires did not budge. No one budged. Some money did trickle in. There would have to be another fund-raising campaign. And there was . . . two years later. In the end it would be the pennies, nickels and dimes of America's working-class men, women and schoolchildren that would provide the money to put the Statue of Liberty on its pedestal.

The design for the great 154-foot-high pedestal took three years to create, from 1881 to 1884. It was the work of Richard Morris Hunt, a well-known American architect with French connections. He had studied in Paris at L'Ecole des Beaux-Arts. Hunt had designed a pedestal that was a tapered form with simple ornamentation and classic overtones. It called for the largest single concrete mass in the world to be faced with stone. It measured 8,281 square feet at the bottom—each of its ground-level sides being 91 feet long—and 4,225 square feet at its top, with sides 65 feet long each. The whole of this massive weight would sit on a foundation nearly 53 feet deep. Pedestal and statue together would stand 305 feet high.

Back in France, the effort to make the Statue of Liberty an American reality continued. On the hundredth anniversary of England's surrender to American and French forces at Yorktown on October 24, 1781, the American ambassador to France, Levi P. Morton, went to the workshops of Gaget, Gauthier. There, on October 24, 1881, he drove the first rivet into a thin copper section of the Statue of Liberty.

By the spring of 1882, craftsmen began to assemble the parts of the statue on the rue de Chazelles, the street next to the workshops. Little by little, Miss Liberty rose feet-first from that Paris street, surrounded by scaffolding and bolted to Eiffel's armature. At the end of 1883, The Statue of Liberty loomed over the roof-

The final design for the pedestal by Richard Morris Hunt, 1884. The inset is Bartholdi's sketch for the pedestal, July 26, 1882, later rejected by Hunt. NPS

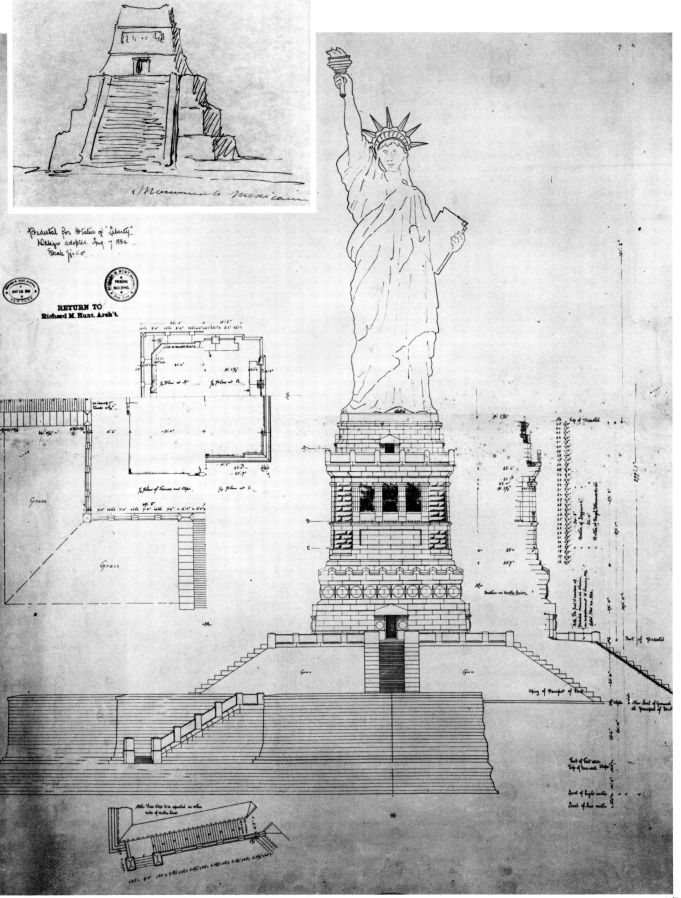

Monuments Mexicain

Pedestal for Statue of "Liberty"
Design adopted Aug 7 1884
Scale ⅛" = 1'. 0"

RETURN TO
Richard M. Hunt, Arch't.

Grass

Grass

Eiffel's armature, Paris, 1881. The inset is
a photograph of Alexandre-Gustave Eiffel. NPS

The bottom section of the Statue of Liberty
after being attached to Eiffel's armature, NPS

49

tops of Paris like an immense goddess. Completed in June 1884, she remained on the rue de Chazelles until January 1885.

On July 4, 1884, the French government officially presented the deed to the Statue of Liberty to the United States. On paper, at least, Miss Liberty now belonged to the American people. The ceremonies were presided over by Ferdinand-Marie de Lesseps. Everyone of note who had a special interest in the project, including Bartholdi, was on hand. Only one was missing. Edouard-René LeFebvre de Laboulaye, who had sparked the entire project, had died shortly before. In making his presentation, Lesseps, now head of the Union Franco-Americaine Committee, spoke glowingly of France's gift to America: "We commit it to your care . . . that it may remain forever the pledge of bonds which shall unite France and the great American nation."

Lesseps announced, too, that his government—the people of France—would pay for the crating and transportation of the Statue of Liberty to New York.

Immediately thereafter, with much encouragement and enthusiasm, the American Committee laid the cornerstone for the pedestal on Bedloe's Island. The six-ton block of Connecticut granite was set in place at two o'clock in the afternoon on a rainy August 5, 1884. The rain was an omen. Within a few weeks of the cornerstone ceremonies, the American Committee ran out of whatever little money it had to begin the pedestal construction. At least one hundred thousand dollars would be needed to complete the pedestal. Americans, rich and poor alike, were not coming forward with money. Most everyone waited for the nation's wealthy or the government to write large checks. Neither did. The public's attitude hardened: Let the French pay for their own pedestal!

On March 16, 1885, an angry Joseph Pulitzer used the editorial pages of his newspaper, the New York *World*, to begin another campaign to raise funds for the pedestal:

The completed Statue of Liberty, Paris, circa 1885,
THE BETTMAN ARCHIVE, INC.

"It would be an irrevocable disgrace to New York City and the American Republic to have France send this splendid gift without our having to provide even so much as a landing place for it. . . . We must raise the money! . . . The $250,000 that the making of the statue cost was paid in by the masses of the French people, by the workingmen, the tradesmen, the shop girls, the artisans—by all, irrespective of class or condition. Let us respond in like manner. . . . It is not a gift from the millionaires of France to the millionaires of America, but a gift of the whole people of France to the whole people of America."

This and subsequent pleas awakened the generosity of the average American. Within five months of Pulitzer's March 1885 editorial, 120,000 people donated $102,000. The Statue of Liberty would have an American pedestal.

Meanwhile, as Pulitzer increased the pressure to raise that $102,000, the Statue of Liberty had arrived in New York. It had been dismantled in January 1885 after having been a Paris landmark for about a year. Carefully numbered, the parts had been put in 214 crates and loaded aboard a French naval freighter, the *Isère,* at the Seine River port of Rouen. The *Isère* sailed on May 21, 1885. Escorted into New York Harbor by French battleships on June 17, the Statue of Liberty had finally arrived. A tumultuous welcome greeted the statue and its escort in Upper New York Bay. Later, a parade was held together with an official reception at City Hall. The statue was unloaded about a month later on Bedloe's Island to await the completion of the pedestal, which was still stalled for lack of money.

With the pedestal funds finally in hand by August 1885, work proceeded, and Bedloe's Island became a beehive of activity. Later, that November, Bartholdi returned to New York for the third time. He only stayed a month. He had come to confer with Major General Charles P. Stone, the project's chief engineer, and

The front page of Pulitzer's newspaper, *The World,* August 11, 1885, NPS

VOL. XXVI., NO. 8,757.　　　NEW YORK, TUESDAY, AUGUST 11, 1885—WITH SUPPLEMENT.　　　PRICE TWO CENTS.

THE SPECTRE IN GRANADA.

A CONDITION MORE HORRIBLE THAN THAT OF NAPLES LAST YEAR.

Cholera Victims Decaying in the Streets—Three Hundred Deaths in Marseilles—Missionaries Massacred in Black Flags in Tonquin—Fatal Fall of an English Railway Station Roof.

THE FUNERAL AS VIEWED IN LONDON.

A Spontaneous Outpouring of People Without a Parallel in History.

MURDERED IN HIS HOME.

A WEALTHY BROOKLYNITE SHOT DOWN BY A HIDDEN FOE.

Albert H. Herrick, Whose Place of Business is at No. 90 William Street, this City, Shot Before He Can Tell Who Fired the Fatal Shot—The Police Without a Clue.

ONE HUNDRED THOUSAND DOLLARS!

TRIUMPHANT COMPLETION OF THE WORLD'S FUND FOR THE LIBERTY PEDESTAL.

Story of the Greatest Popular Subscription Ever Raised in America—How the Republic Was Saved from Lasting Disgrace—An Event for Patriotic Citizens to Rejoice Over—A Roll of Honor Bearing the Names of 120,000 Generous Patriots—The Flags of France and the American Union Floating in Sisterly Sympathy—Over $3,500 Received Yesterday—The Grand Total Foots Up $102,006.39—A Generous Lady Pays $130 for the Washington Cent.

BY AUTHORITY OF THE AMERICAN COMMITTEE OF THE
STATUE OF LIBERTY.

Richard Morris Hunt, the architect. Their meetings concerned the final assembly of the statue on the pedestal. By April 1886, the work of mounting the statue on the now-completed pedestal had begun. And by October it was all done. Three men had contributed their genius in making the Statue of Liberty a monumental work of art not only for America but for the entire world:

FRÉDÉRIC-AUGUSTE BARTHOLDI, sculptor, the artist who not only created the statue itself but successfully promoted the idea to America.

ALEXANDRE-GUSTAVE EIFFEL, structural engineer, without whose perfectly designed armature the colossal Statue of Liberty would have been impossible.

RICHARD MORRIS HUNT, architect, whose elegantly designed pedestal did justice to an already monumental work of art.

Bartholdi arrived with the French delegation on October 25, 1886, three days before the unveiling ceremonies. Although the harbor was thick with fog, his ship, the *Bretagne,* easily found her berth. There, the party transferred to a small boat to cruise the harbor and perhaps glimpse the new American landmark through the mist. The dinners, parties and ceremonies that awaited Bartholdi, including all the honors that were heaped upon him, were wonderful and memorable excitements, enough to last a lifetime. But Bartholdi expressed his true and deep feelings when he said to a group of reporters, "The dream of my life is accomplished."

With the dedication and unveiling on that wet day of October 28, 1886, the Statue of Liberty became a property of the United

Richard Morris Hunt's pedestal for
the Statue of Liberty, 1886, NPS

States government to be maintained by the Lighthouse Board. The Lighthouse Board remained in charge of the statue until 1902. After that and until 1933, it was maintained by the War Department. The National Park Service of the Department of the Interior took charge of the island and statue in 1933.

Fifty years after the Statue of Liberty was first dedicated, another dedication ceremony took place. It had been some time since Miss Liberty shone like a new copper penny. Now her copper structure had a bluish-greenish cast, or patina. Water, sun, air, heat, cold and other natural elements had changed the character and chemistry of the copper.

Beneath the statue's graceful pose, President Franklin Delano Roosevelt spoke of liberty and reaffirmed American ideals on October 28, 1936. His words echoed against the background of the Great Depression, when employment and opportunity evaporated for millions of Americans. Soon, the sound of marching feet in Europe would engulf the entire world in war.

Liberty's torch would not glow during America's participation in World War II (1941–1945), since New York was blacked out for fear of attack. But after the war it would again cast a yellowish light in every kind of weather. The torch glowed brightly during the 1970s, but it was obvious that the Statue of Liberty, now approaching its hundredth birthday, was in need of repairs and some sprucing up.

During the 1970s a campaign was begun among all Americans, including schoolchildren, to raise funds to restore the Statue of Liberty, Liberty Island and neighboring Ellis Island. (Ellis Island was the reception station for newly arrived immigrants for sixty-two years, from 1892 until 1954.) These landmarks held tremendous meaning for the millions of Americans whose first glimpse of the New World began in New York Harbor. Recognizing the importance of these monuments, the Statue of Liberty/Ellis Island

President Franklin Delano Roosevelt speaking on Bedloe's
Island at the 50th anniversary ceremony, October 28, 1936, NPS

Centennial Commission has worked hard to generate funds, support and enthusiasm for restoring the Statue of Liberty in time for rededication on October 28, 1986. When the restoration scaffolding is removed and Liberty's torch is lit again, it will glow more brightly than ever before.

The lighting of the torch had been a problem from the very beginning of the statue's existence. Electric lighting had just been invented by Thomas Alva Edison in 1879 as the Statue of Liberty was being created. The torch itself was not electrified until a month or two following the dedication in 1886. Until then the torch had been made of opaque copper sheets. The U.S. Army Engineers cut windows out of the copper, installed light bulbs inside and hoped to produce a lighted effect. The result was disappointing. In 1916, the torch was redesigned. The copper sheets were replaced by a series of glass windows. The lighting was vastly improved. Still, the lit torch did not have the brightness that the Union Franco-Americaine Committee (and Bartholdi) envisioned as one day radiating "on the far flung waves of the ocean." Over the next sixty years, various lighting systems were installed in the torch. Each was an improvement over the previous one. By 1976, the torch glowed brighter than ever. But with the restoration, the torch will no longer be a patchwork of clear glass covering a beacon lamp. Instead, it will be a series of gold sheets floodlit from around the torch's balcony.

And still fastened to the pedestal's interior wall will be the modest bronze plaque that was placed there without fanfare in 1903. On the plaque is a poem by poet Emma Lazarus that speaks eloquently of America's purpose. Emma Lazarus was asked to write such a poem in 1883 as part of the campaign to raise funds for the Statue of Liberty pedestal. Both Emma Lazarus and Joseph Pulitzer were Jewish. Alive in their minds during the 1880s were the bloody massacres of Jews living in Russia, forcing many

to flee for their lives and to come to America. The Statue of Liberty had deep meaning for them—as deep as Bartholdi's passion for his lost town of Colmar. And so Emma Lazarus, New York born and bred, wrote "The New Colossus" in despair and in protest of tyranny. She died in 1887, never to know that her poem would become an emotional inspiration for millions of immigrants to the United States. But Bartholdi would live to know. He died in 1904.

Not like the brazen giant of Greek fame,
With conquering limbs astride from land to land;
Here at our sea-washed, sunset gates shall stand
A mighty woman with a torch, whose flame
Is the imprisoned lightning, and her name
Mother of Exiles. From her beacon hand
Glows world-wide welcome; her mild eyes command
The air-bridged harbor that twin cities frame.
"Keep, ancient lands, your storied pomp!" cries she
With silent lips. "Give me your tired, your poor,
Your huddled masses yearning to breathe free,
The wretched refuse of your teeming shore,
Send these, the homeless, tempest-tost to me,
I lift my lamp beside the golden door!"

INDEX

The document of the Franco-American Union presenting the Statue of
Liberty as a gift to the American people, July 4, 1884, NPS

NPS

The author would like to thank Mr. Won H. Kim, the librarian at the American Museum of Immigration on Liberty Island, for his help. The credit line NPS by many of the photographs in this book is an abbreviation for National Park Service: Statue of Liberty, N.M./American Museum of Immigration.

109811

Copyright © 1985 by Leonard Everett Fisher
All rights reserved
Printed in the United States of America
Designed by Leonard Everett Fisher
First Edition

11/85 12.95 BT/City

Library of Congress Cataloging in Publication Data

Fisher, Leonard Everett.
The Statue of Liberty.

Includes index.

SUMMARY: Recounts the history of one of the largest monuments in the world, including how it was executed in France, shipped to America, and erected in New York Harbor.
    1. Statue of Liberty (New York, N.Y.)—Juvenile literature.   2. New York (N.Y.)—Buildings, structures, etc.   [1. Statue of Liberty (New York, N.Y.)
2. National monuments.   3. Statues]   I. Title.
F128.64.L6F575   1985   974.7′1   85-42878
ISBN 0-8234-0586-9